Sweet Dried Apples

A Vietnamese Wartime Childhood

Rosemary Breckler

Illustrated by Deborah Kogan Ray

Houghton Mifflin Company

Boston   1996

For information about this and other Houghton Mifflin trade and reference books and
multimedia products, visit The Bookstore at Houghton Mifflin on the World Wide Web at
http://www.hmco.com/trade/.

Manufactured in the United States of America

Book design by David Saylor
The text of this book is set in 16-point Cochin.
The illustrations were painted with transparent watercolor
and watercolor pencil on 140 lb. Arches hot press paper.

BVG 10 9 8 7 6 5 4 3 2 1

LIBRARY OF CONGRESS CATALOGING-IN-PUBLICATION DATA
Breckler, Rosemary
    Sweet dried apples/Rosemary Breckler; illustrated by Deborah Kogan Ray.   p.   cm.
    Summary: A Vietnamese child remembers wartime and her relationship with her grandfather,
the village herb doctor.
    ISBN: 0-395-73570-X
    1. Vietnamese Conflict, 1961-1975—Juvenile fiction. [1. Vietnamese Conflict,
1961-1975—Fiction. 2. Grandfathers —Fiction.] I. Ray, Deborah Kogan, ill. II. Title.
    PZ7.B744Sw   1996   [E]—dc20   95-518   CIP AC

To my granddaughter, Cassie Marie Lasater.
She keeps my mind turning cartwheels.
—R. K. B.

To Lady—a woman of conscience,
who has known Vietnam in war and peace.
—D. K. R.

The sun was still sleeping when I opened my eyes. Across the room my little brother, Duc, rolled to the edge of his mat. In the silent house I heard Ma's soft footsteps.

Ma walked in and sat down. "Ba has gone to war," she said. Her voice sounded as if it had a crack in it. The war was far from our village. I wondered when Ba would come home.

That afternoon Duc and I were up in our favorite
guava tree when I spotted someone on the village road.
"Duc! Isn't that Ong Noi?"

Ong Noi was our revered elder, our father's father.
Though we visited him on all holidays, he seldom came
to our house. In one basket of his shoulder yoke we could
see his clothes. In the other was a jumble of bottles and
packages, the medicines he used in his work as the village
herb doctor.

A few minutes later Ong Noi was looking up at us.
"So! My grandchildren are monkeys!" We scrambled
down the tree to bow before him.

"Your Ba has joined the soldiers," he said. "Now I
will look after you until he returns." He pulled a slender
bamboo stick from his medicine basket and shook it in
front of us. "You see?" he said, pretending to be stern.
"I have come prepared to help you grow straight as
this stick."

How we teased him by doing little naughty things!
Each time, he waved his stick at us and said, "Be good,
or be sorry."

"Oh please, sir," we pleaded, bowing, "do not swat us."
Of course, he never did.

We could not resist the sweet dried apples Ong Noi
used to flavor his bitter herb remedies. He had to pay a
good price for the imported apples and kept them high
on top of our tall armoire. But that did not stop us.

Ong Noi taught us how to gather wild herbs, bark, and roots in the cool green forest. "Here! Here, sir," we happily called when we made a good find. He always rewarded us with a loving pat.

As a treat, Ong Noi took us along to market. He
carried his yoke with its swinging baskets. Duc and I
carried plastic tote bags for special goods, like Ong Noi's
sweet dried apples.

Months passed and we heard constant roaring in the sky. Booming noises echoed from far off. People hurried along the road's open spaces, trying to keep under the umbrella of trees.

Ong Noi built a new schoolroom for Ma just outside our back door. Frightened mothers brought their children to her school instead of going to the village. Ong Noi always seemed to be listening for something. "Be quiet, please!" he would say, interrupting our noisy games.

Duc and I found a secret place to play. Grasses and wildflowers had quickly grown around the air space under the school building and we felt sure no one would find us there.

Once we stayed in our hideout while Ong Noi called for us. When we got tired of hiding, we scrambled out and walked slowly toward him, laughing. Ong Noi did not smile. "You must never wander from home!" he warned us.

Then one night Ong Noi took all of his medicines and his apples and tied them up in little pouches which he hung from his belt. He drew each of us to him. "Tonight I must make a journey. Be good. Listen to your mother. Be sorry if you make her worry!"

We watched him disappear into the dark. We could hear rumbling and cracking sounds in the distance. "The war is coming this way," Ma said, holding us close.

The next day I said to Duc, "Let's have a surprise for
Ong Noi when he comes back." We made a bunch of little
pouches and went out each morning to look for herbs.
Soon we had a nice supply in our hideout.

Dried apples were expensive, so Duc and I picked
guavas instead. We chopped them up and spread them in
the sun to dry into sweet chewy bits, like candy.

After many weeks, Ong Noi returned.
His face looked like ashes. He was so thin
that I could hardly tell he was our grandfather.
"The war is coming here! Hide under the
schoolroom," he said and fell to the floor.

I touched him. His face was hot. We pulled
him into the air space. Ma brought her grass
bed-mat from the house and helped Ong Noi
onto it.

The night suddenly became bright with fire. Everything around us seemed to be burning.

Ma held Duc and me tightly in her arms. Ong Noi's head rested in her lap. "My medicines," he moaned. "Without my medicines, the people in the village will die!"

In the morning, we crawled out to a black world. The bamboo trees were gone. All around us were mountains that we had never seen. No birds sang in the sky. The rice fields were ashes. We all wept.

Duc and I showed Ong Noi our store of herbs. He thanked us, his eyes full of respect. Over the next few days, he helped the people who came begging for medicine. Then, exhausted, having saved none for himself, our grandfather fell asleep forever. We made Ong Noi's eternity blanket from a mound of flower-strewn dirt.

"We must leave," Ma said. "Ba will know how to find us." She opened a drawer in the armoire and pulled out a black silk bag containing our money. She tied the bag around her waist under her oldest, fullest teacher's smock. I wrapped the last guava pieces in a thin cloth.

As soon as it was dark, we joined neighbors all heading east, toward a sliver of rising moon. "To market," we said if an enemy soldier asked us where we were headed. We crept along like shadows, resting in tunnels near burned houses.

Then one night a truck driven by our own soldiers brought us to the sea. A small fishing boat waited to carry us out to a large ship. Ma carefully untied her silk bag and paid the fee. We crowded onto the boat.
Soon there was nothing but water.

Someday, I promised myself, I will find a way back. I will light fragrant incense so Ong Noi will know that I am there. I will burn paper money so its smoke will rise up to him and he can buy comforts. I will bring him sweet dried apples instead of flowers.

DATE DUE

APR 1 4 '99			
OCT 0 4 '00			
MAR 3 1 2002			
NOV 2 9 2010			
AUG 2 9 2011			
GAYLORD			PRINTED IN U.S.A.